The Kidnapped Kitten

Other titles by Holly Webb

The Snow Bear
The Reindeer Girl
The Winter Wolf

Animal Stories:

My Naughty Little Puppy:

The Kidnapped Kitten

Holly Webb
Illustrated by Sophy Williams

stripes

For Lizzie

For more information about Holly Webb visit:
www.hollywebbanimalstories.com

STRIPES PUBLISHING
An imprint of Little Tiger Press
1 The Coda Centre, 189 Munster Road,
London SW6 6AW

A paperback original
First published in Great Britain in 2014

Text copyright © Holly Webb, 2014
Illustrations copyright © Sophy Williams, 2014
Author photograph copyright © Nigel Bird
My Naughty Little Puppy illustration copyright © Kate Pankhurst

ISBN: 978-1-84715-422-4

A CIP catalogue record for this book is available
from the British Library.

Printed and bound in the UK.

10 9 8 7 6 5 4

Chapter One

"Laura! Laura!" Tia waved, as she rushed down their street on the way home from school.

Her neighbour stood up and waved back. Laura was planting something in her front garden and her beautiful cat, Charlie, was sitting next to her, staring suspiciously at the turned-over earth.

Tia ran up and leaned over the wall,

and her little sister, Christy, followed, panting, "You went too fast for me!"

"Sorry," said Tia, taking her sister's hand. "Laura, guess what?"

Laura smiled. "What? Something good, it sounds like."

Tia nodded. "The best. Mum and Dad say we can have a cat!"

Christy did a twirly dance. "A cat! A cat!" she sang.

"Oh, that's so exciting." Laura beamed at them. "You'll be brilliant cat owners. You were great when you came with your mum to feed Charlie while I was away. He looked quite grumpy when I got back – I don't think I was fussing over him as much as you two were." She looked up in surprise as Charlie suddenly pounced on the pile of earth. "Oh, Charlie! Stop it! You don't want it, you silly cat."

"What is it?" Tia tried to see what Charlie was patting at with his paw.

"A worm. No, don't eat it! Euurrgh!" Laura picked up Charlie and dusted the soil off his paws, and the worm made a quick getaway.

"He eats *worms*?" Christy peered over the wall at Charlie.

Laura grinned. "He eats everything. Especially things that wriggle. Bengals are a bit like that. Really nosy."

"Charlie's a special breed of cat then?" Tia asked thoughtfully. "I've never seen another cat that looks quite like him. He's like a leopard."

"Exactly." Laura nodded and put Charlie on top of the wall so the girls could admire him. He sat down with his tail wrapped around his paws and his nose in the air, posing. "Bengals are bred from leopard cats – little wild cats that live in Asia. Leopard cats are spotty like big leopards. But you can get Bengals with swirly stripes as well."

Tia reached out her hand to Charlie and made kissy noises at him.

Charlie gazed back at her. He had his eyes half-closed, which made him look very snooty, but Tia thought it was actually because he was a bit embarrassed about not being allowed to eat worms.

He eyed her thoughtfully for a few more seconds, then stood up and stepped delicately along the wall to allow her to stroke him.

"You're the nicest cat ever," Tia murmured. She glanced up at Laura. "You know, his fur's almost sparkly when you look at him in the sunshine."

"It's called glitter." Laura nodded. "Lots of Bengal cats have it." She rubbed Charlie's ears. "It's actually because some of his fur is see-through, but it looks like he's covered in gold dust. He's a precious boy."

"Hi, Laura! I hope the girls aren't bothering you." Tia and Christy's mum hurried up.

"No, it's fine. They were just telling me their exciting news." Laura smiled. "If you get a cat, then they can both sit in our front windows and stare at each other!"

Tia giggled, imagining it. Laura's

house was just across the road from theirs, so the two cats really would be able to see each other. Charlie liked to sit on the windowsill and look out. Tia always waved at him on her way past.

Tia ran her hand down Charlie's satiny back again. "Mum! Could we have a cat like Charlie?"

Her mum reached out to scratch Charlie under the chin. "I'm sorry, Tia, but I don't think so. Charlie's beautiful, but he's a pedigree cat. He must have been really expensive." She glanced at Laura, looking a bit embarrassed. "Sorry!"

Laura made a face. "No, don't worry. He *was* expensive. But I'd wanted a Bengal cat for ages. I just loved the way they looked, and I'd read about what funny characters they are. So I saved up for him."

"We'll probably go to the Cats Protection League and see if they have any kittens available," Tia's mum explained to Laura. "Even though you are gorgeous, aren't you?" She made coaxing noises at Charlie, and he did his superior face back again.

"Lucy got Mittens from the Cats Protection League. Lucy's my best friend from school," Tia put in. "She's got a really cute black and white cat, with little white mittens on the fronts of her paws. It's all right, Mittens isn't as beautiful as you," she added to Charlie, who was looking outraged. "Sometimes I think he understands everything we say," she told Laura.

"That's the thing with Bengals," Laura said. "They're very clever. Lots of them have tricks, like opening doors – Charlie can do that. But it means they can be quite difficult to look after. When they get bored, they can be naughty. I wouldn't be able to have Charlie if I didn't work at home. He'd be lonely if I was out all day."

"Cats need company," Tia's mum agreed. "But I only work afternoons, so we should be all right." Tia's mum worked part-time in the office at Tia and Christy's school. "Anyway, we should leave you in peace. Come on, girls."

"Bye, Charlie." Tia gave him one last loving stroke. "See you tomorrow on the way to school!"

"You don't mind that we can't have

a cat like Charlie?" her mum asked, as she unlocked the front door.

Tia turned round and hugged her. "No! I just want a cat of our own, that's all. Maybe a black and white cat, like Lucy's? Will we be able to choose between lots of cats?"

"I'm not sure…" her mum said. "I'll have to call the Cats Protection League. Lucy's mum was telling me about Mittens, and I think she came from a lady who just had a few kittens living in her house. I don't think the Cats Protection League has one big shelter."

"That's probably nicer for the cats," Tia pointed out, as she took off her shoes.

"When's our cat coming?" Christy asked. Christy was only four, and she didn't really understand about the time things took.

"In a little while, I promise," Mum said, and Tia gave a little sigh of happiness. Hopefully they wouldn't have to wait too long…

"Tia! Tia!"

They were on their way to school, and Tia had been daydreaming about what sort of cat they might get. She jumped when Laura shouted after her.

Laura was at her front door, with Charlie weaving himself possessively around her ankles. "Oh, I'm glad I caught you! Is your mum around?"

"She's a bit further up the road, chasing after Christy," Tia explained.

"I don't want to make you late for school, but I really wanted to let you know…"

Tia stared at Laura, not really sure what she was talking about.

"Sorry! I'll start at the beginning. The lady who bred Charlie called me last night – I'd sent her a photo of him, and she was ringing to say thank you. And she mentioned she's got a Bengal kitten for sale!"

"But we can't—" Tia started to say. Mum was right. They really couldn't afford a pedigree cat.

"Oh, I know, but that's the thing. This kitten won't be very expensive.

She's got a bent tail. She's still gorgeous, but it's what's called a fault. It means she can't be in a cat show, and no one would want her to have kittens, as they might have bent tails too. So I thought I'd tell you, just in case you want to go and see her. I expect lots of people will be keen to buy her – sometimes people wait ages for a Bengal kitten. I wrote it all down for you." Laura darted back into the house and returned with a scrap of paper. "Here, give this to your mum. It's the breeder's phone number."

Tia looked down at the piece of paper. *Glimmershine Bengals*, it said, *Helen Mason*, and a phone number. But somehow, for Tia, the scribbly writing seemed to say, *Your very own kitten...*

Chapter Two

"Are we sure about getting a Bengal kitten?" Dad asked, looking at the Glimmershine website. Tia had found it for him on his phone, so he could read it while he ate his toast. "It says here about them being *very individual characters*. That sounds like the kind of thing teachers say when they don't want to say *just plain naughty*."

Tia giggled. "Laura said Charlie's a bit like that."

"Mmmm. But he's so friendly with you and Christy," Mum said. "Some cats aren't that keen on children."

"Laura said Bengals can be naughty when they get bored and lonely," Tia added. "But Mum's around in the mornings, and we can play with the kitten after school."

"I suppose so," Dad agreed. "Well, there's no harm going to see this kitten, anyway. What time did she say we should come over?"

"Any time from ten." Mum looked at her watch. "We should probably get going, actually. It's about half an hour away."

Tia jumped up from the table, nearly

tipping over her cereal bowl. Even though it was the weekend, she'd been up since six.

"Slow down," Dad chuckled.

"Sorry…" Tia said. "It's just so exciting!"

The car journey seemed to take far longer than half an hour. Tia was much too jittery to read a book or listen to music. They might actually be getting their kitten! She wriggled delightedly at the thought.

The house they pulled up at looked surprisingly ordinary – apart from a small sign, with a drawing of a cat on it. Somehow Tia had expected something different, although she wasn't quite sure what. She followed her mum and dad up the path, feeling oddly disappointed.

Then Christy clutched at her arm. "Tia, look!" She was pointing at the window on one side of the front door.

The windowsill was lined with kittens. They were all sitting watching the girls walk up the path, their ears pricked up curiously.

"So many of them!" Tia gasped. They seemed to be different ages, too – some of them were much bigger than the others. She tried to count them, but Dad had rung the doorbell, and the kittens clearly heard it. They hurried to jump down from the windowsill – there had to be a chair or something underneath it, as they were all queuing to get down. Except that they didn't queue very nicely, they were all pushing and barging into each other.

Someone had answered the door, but Tia and Christy hardly noticed – they were too busy watching the kittens.

"If you come in, you'll be able to see them even better!" A grey-haired lady looked round the door, smiling.

Tia went pink and hurried in, hauling Christy after her.

The door to the room with the window was closed, and Tia could hear squeaks and bumps from behind it. She stared at it hopefully, while Mum asked about the kitten Laura had mentioned.

The grey-haired lady – Helen, Tia remembered she was called – nodded. "She's a lovely little thing – she'll make a very friendly pet." She beamed at the girls. "So would you like to meet them all, then?"

Tia just nodded, she couldn't even speak. Christy jumped up and down as Helen carefully opened the door.

"I have to open it slowly," she explained. "They get so excited about people visiting, and they *will* stand there just behind the door. I'll catch their paws if I'm not careful." She bent down as the door opened and scooped up a small kitten with golden-brown fur and the most beautiful leopardy spots, who was making a run for it.

"There's always one," she told Tia, "and actually this is the little lady you've come to see."

Tia gasped as the kitten peered down at her. She had enormous round eyes, not green or yellowy, like most cats, but a soft, turquoise blue. Her ears were massive, too, and she had a great long trail of white whiskers.

"Come on in, and we'll shut the door before they all try and escape," Helen said.

The room had been a dining room,
Tia realized. It still had the table
and chairs, but now there were soft,
padded baskets, food bowls and litter
trays everywhere.

"It's a kitten room," Christy cried, looking round. "There's so many!"

"Eleven of them," Helen said. "Two litters. The smaller ones are ten weeks old, and the bigger ones are twelve weeks. Ready to go to their new homes."

"Oh…" Tia breathed. "She's old enough to come to us already?" She was still staring at the pretty dappled kitten in Helen's arms. "If she wants to, I mean," she added. Somehow it seemed quite clear that it wasn't only her decision. The blue-green eyes peering over Helen's arm were determined.

Helen nodded. "Why don't you try and stroke her?" she said, lowering her arms a little to make it easier for Tia to reach the kitten.

Very gently, Tia held out her fingers, and the kitten sniffed them thoughtfully. Tia rubbed her hand over the kitten's silky head. "Oh, she's so soft. Like satin."

The kitten let out a mighty purr, a huge noise from something so small, and Tia burst out laughing. The kitten laid back her ears, her eyes getting even huger, and Tia gulped. "I'm sorry, I didn't mean to scare you," she murmured. But the kitten purred again, and Helen slowly held her out to Tia.

"See if she'll let you hold her," she said quietly.

Tia glanced nervously at Mum. But Mum gave an encouraging smile. "She does seem to like you, Tia. You're so good at being gentle."

Tia carefully took the kitten from Helen. "Look at her gorgeous spots," she whispered to Mum.

Dad and Christy were crouched down by the dining table looking at one of the smaller kittens, who was perched on a chair. "She's not quite like Charlie though, is she? Her spots are in rings. Like pawprints!"

"She is lovely," Helen said. "You aren't worried about her tail, then?"

"Oh! I forgot." Tia peered round the little kitten, who was snuggling into the front of her top. It looked pretty much like a normal tail to her, only a little bit bent at the tip. "I love her tail," she said firmly. "It's so dark! Nearly black, and the rest of her looks like – like honeycomb toffee!"

"She does," Mum nodded.

"So … we can really have her?" Tia asked hopefully. She giggled as the kitten hooked tiny claws into her top and started to mountaineer up her shoulder and round her neck until she was standing with her front paws on one shoulder and her back paws on the other, like a furry scarf.

Mum glanced over at Dad, who nodded. "I think she's perfect."

The kitten purred in Tia's ear, as though she agreed.

Tia had hoped they might be able to take the kitten home with them, but Mum and Dad said they needed to get everything ready first. Tia supposed they were right. They didn't even have a cat carrier. So after they'd finally coaxed Christy away from the tiny kittens, they stopped off at the pet shop on the way home.

"Can we buy some toys as well?" Tia asked. "They had lots of toys at Helen's house. I don't want the kitten to be bored at ours."

"What are the chances of that?" Dad laughed. "I don't think her paws are going to touch the floor."

"A couple of toys," Mum agreed.

"But we're not going mad with them, Tia."

"I've got my birthday money from Gran still," Tia pointed out. "I could use that." She stood in front of the cat toys, looking at catnip fish, laser pointers and jingly balls. What should she get? Tia could imagine the kitten loving them all.

She was just trying out a clockwork mouse, when a poster hanging at the end of the aisle caught her eye. It was for the Cats Protection League, asking for donations to feed all the stray cats they took in. Tia looked at it thoughtfully. If her family had adopted a kitten from there, they would have made a donation...

She looked down at her basket and put back the feathery cat dancer and the catnip monkey. She could make a bunch of feathers, and Mum had lots of knitting wool. She would buy the mouse, but that was all. The rest of her money she dropped into the collection box at the till. The bag the lady gave her to take home was very light, but Tia didn't mind.

Chapter Three

The kitten let out a despairing wail. She hated being shut up in the cat carrier. It was too small and it smelled funny, and she seemed to have been in it for ages. But then there was a clicking noise and the door swung open.

The girl was looking in at her now, the one who had stroked her and fussed over her. The kitten nosed forward cautiously. The girl rubbed her ears gently, and the kitten stepped out of the carrier and climbed on to her lap, which was beautifully still after the car ride. Then she peered around worriedly. This wasn't the place she knew, and there seemed to be an awful lot of people and movement and noise.

"She's so quiet," Tia said, as Dad crouched next to her and stroked the kitten.

"She's just not sure what's going on, poor little thing. She'll probably go and explore in a minute."

But the kitten didn't. She didn't go and try out the padded basket they'd bought, or drink from her smart new bowl, or chase after her clockwork mouse. When Tia had to get up and have dinner, the kitten darted off her lap and hid round the side of the cat carrier. She didn't want to go right back in it, but somehow it felt safe. She could have gone with the girl to the table, but there were too many people over there. *Safer to stay by the carrier,* she thought.

"I want her to play with me!" Christy wailed, pushing her plate away. "She sat on Tia for ages! Why won't she play?"

"She will," Mum promised. "She just needs to get used to us, Christy."

"Anyway, we need to think about what to call her," Dad pointed out.

Tia peered at the cat carrier. She could see white whiskers sticking out round the corner of it. The kitten was so pretty, she needed a pretty sort of name – like Rosie, or Coco – except that sounded too much like a poodle.

"What about Milly?" she suggested. "She looks like a Milly, I think."

"Milly…" Mum nodded. "I like it."

After dinner, Tia crouched down by the carrier. She didn't want to scare the kitten, she just wanted to show her that someone was there. The kitten peeped out at her every so often.

Tia had been sitting there for a good twenty minutes when Milly finally edged her way further out from behind the carrier. Tia held her breath. Would she come right out?

"Tia! Are you still there?" Mum asked, coming into the kitchen.

The kitten whisked back behind the carrier with a flick of her tail.

"It's bedtime. Don't worry, Milly will be fine. Dad and I will keep checking on her."

Tia trailed upstairs reluctantly. It felt so mean to leave the little kitten all by herself. She lay in the dark listening to Christy breathing in the bottom bunk, too worried to sleep.

At least she thought she was. She woke suddenly from a dream that she couldn't really remember, except that it hadn't been good. She had been searching for something...

Tia sat up in bed. It was late. Mum and Dad had surely gone to bed – she couldn't hear their voices or the TV.

She could hear something, though. A sad, thin little wail. Yes, there it was again. The kitten!

Tia slid down her bunkbed ladder and padded as quietly as she could out on to the landing and down the stairs. She opened the kitchen door and whispered, "Puss puss... Milly... It's so dark, I'll have to put the light on. Don't be surprised, all right?" She closed the door behind her and clicked on the light, blinking in the sudden glare. She'd expected to see the kitten dart back behind her carrier, or maybe she would be in her basket – but Tia couldn't see her anywhere.

"Milly?" she murmured, turning

slowly in the middle of the room.
"Where are you?"

She has to be here, Tia told herself.
*I heard her. She can't have got out of
the cat flap.* Dad had put the cat flap
in, but they had kept it locked – Milly
wouldn't be allowed to go out until
she'd had all her vaccinations. She was
hiding, that was all. *Where would a
kitten like to hide?* Tia wondered.

The oilcloth covering the kitchen
table moved slightly, as though there
was a draught – but all the windows
were closed. Tia smiled and crouched
down under the table. There, in the
dim light under the cloth, a pair of
blue-green eyes shone out at her. Milly
was sitting on a stool, with the cloth
tucked round her like a little tent.

"Hello," Tia whispered.

The kitten stared back at her, and Tia settled herself against the leg of the table. "I'll sit here," she said sleepily. "Just to make sure you're OK."

She was half asleep when she felt little paws padding at her leg, and then Milly scrambled on to her lap and curled herself into a tiny ball.

"Tia! What are you doing under there?" Christy squeaked. "You weren't in your bed – I came to find you!"

Tia blinked. The light was still on and the kitchen seemed very bright. "Is it morning?" she muttered.

"Yes! Did you sleep down here all night?"

"No… I came down in the middle sometime. Owww, I'm all stiff." Tia tried to stretch out her legs without disturbing Milly, who was blinking at her owlishly.

Christy creeped under the table to join them and stroked Milly's back, following the direction of the fur the way Tia had taught her. "I'm so glad she's ours," she said.

"I know," Tia agreed. "I can't wait

to tell Lucy all about her at school tomorrow."

"Oh, hello, you two – you three, I mean." Mum peered under the oilcloth. "Did you come down early to play with her?"

Tia gave Christy a look and nodded. It was better that Mum didn't know she'd been downstairs half the night...

After that first night, Milly settled in quickly. She didn't stay confined to the kitchen for long – she was far too nosy. She missed her old home and all her brothers and sisters, but now she had a whole house to explore. She explored it properly, too – every surface, every shelf, every cupboard. She wasn't big enough to climb the stairs at first, but whenever Tia and Christy were home, they were happy to carry her. And by the time she had been living with Tia's family for a month, she was big enough to scramble up them by herself.

Milly's favourite place was Tia and Christy's room. It was full of toys to chase and boxes to wriggle in and out of. She was also fascinated by the ladder to Tia's top bunk. Tia had carried her up there, but Milly wanted to be able to climb it on her own.

"What are you doing, kitten?" Tia said, laughing as she watched Milly from her desk. She was trying to do her homework, but Milly kept stealing her pencils and burying them under the bed.

Milly put her front paws on the first step – the ladder had flat, wide rungs, and it was easy enough to jump on to one. She managed to jump from the first step to the second. But then she wobbled and slid, and had to make a flying leap down on to Christy's bed instead. Then she went prowling off through the soft toys, pretending that was what she had meant to do all along.

Tia wished she could play with Milly, but she had to finish her homework first.

It wasn't until Christy came upstairs and let out a piercing shriek that Tia realized what Milly had been doing. One of Christy's favourite toys was a

feathery owl that Dad
had brought back
for her from a
work trip. It
always sat propped
up at the side of her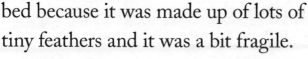
bed because it was made up of lots of
tiny feathers and it was a bit fragile.

"Owly! She's eaten Owly!" Christy
howled.

Milly sat in the middle of the bed,
looking rather confused. Christy did
burst out crying every so often, she'd
got used to that now. But she was
being very loud and she was stamping
about. Milly spat out a mouthful of
the interesting feathers and slunk to
the end of the bed, making for Tia.

"Whatever's the matter?" Mum said,

rushing in. "Oh my goodness. Christy, I'm sorry, sweetheart."

"He's all eaten and ruined…" Christy sobbed.

"Tia, how on earth could you have let Milly do that?" Mum asked.

"I didn't see! I was doing my homework. Sorry, Christy…" Tia picked Milly up, looking guiltily at her little sister. "Maybe we can glue the feathers back on."

"You shouldn't cuddle her," Christy growled. "She's a bad cat!"

"Oh no, she isn't! She didn't know."

Milly snuggled closer into Tia's school jumper, not liking the angry voices.

"You're scaring her!" Tia said, and Christy wailed again.

"I don't care! She broke Owly!"

"Take that cat downstairs, Tia," Mum snapped. "Honestly, after the pavlova yesterday as well. I never thought a kitten could be so much trouble."

"I wish we had a kitten that didn't eat things!" Christy gulped.

Tia hurried down the stairs with Milly in her arms. "You are silly," she muttered. "I love you climbing about and getting into everything, but the pavlova was a disaster."

Mum had been making a lovely pudding to take to a friend's house, and she'd left it out on the counter while she answered the door. She came back to find a very happy cat, and a lot less whipped cream on top of the pavlova. Mum had had to buy a pudding instead, although Tia was sure it would have been all right if Mum had just moved the raspberries around a bit.

"I think you'd better try and be perfectly behaved for the next few days," she told Milly, as she put her in her basket. "You're definitely not Mum or Christy's favourite cat right now."

"You don't think there's anything I can do about Milly, then?" Tia asked Laura, sipping at her juice. It was the weekend, and she'd popped over to get some advice on Milly's naughty tricks.

Laura shook her head slowly. "Not much. Just make her get down every time you see her somewhere she shouldn't be. A lot of it's simply that she's a kitten. She will get better as she gets older. Charlie used to knock things over all the time, but he doesn't do quite so much climbing now."

Tia sighed. It didn't look like there was an easy answer. "I guess I'm lucky she hasn't really spoiled anything of mine yet. Well, she did eat my sandwiches yesterday while Mum was doing my packed lunch. But that's not the same as Owly. Christy is still really upset. She says we should take Milly back and get a better-behaved cat."

"I suppose the thing to do is make sure anything precious is put away," Laura said. "And shut the doors if there are rooms you don't want her in."

"Mmmm," Tia agreed. "It's just Christy *never* shuts doors."

"Milly might learn to open them anyway. I wouldn't be surprised. Actually, Tia, I'm glad you came over," Laura said, reaching over to a pile of newspapers on one of the kitchen chairs. "I was going to talk to your mum or dad. Do you know if they've seen this?" She folded the newspaper over and showed a headline to Tia – CATNAPPERS STEAL PRECIOUS PETS.

"No!" Tia looked at it in horror. "Why are they stealing them?"

"To sell." Laura was frowning. "It's because pedigree cats are so expensive. The thieves steal them and then sell them for less than you'd pay at a breeder. I'm sure most of the people don't realize the cats are stolen. The thing is, this

article particularly mentions Bengals.
Because they're so fashionable. And
I know that one lady who has one of
Charlie's littermates caught someone
trying to tempt her cat out of her garden.
She doesn't live all that far from here."

Tia jumped up from the table. "I'm
really sorry, Laura, but I have to go
home. Milly's allowed out of her cat
flap now. What if someone's trying
to steal her this minute?"

Chapter Four

Laura tried to tell Tia that it was unlikely anyone would try and steal Milly, and she hadn't meant to scare her. She was still letting Charlie go out, but only when she was around to keep an eye on him. "Just to be safe," she explained.

Tia calmed down enough to finish her juice. But she refused a biscuit, and as she hurried back home she couldn't help keeping an eye out for cat thieves. *What would they look like, though?*

Tia went down the side of her house to the back garden. Milly loved it out there. She bounced in and out of the plants, and spied on the bird table. Tia had noticed that only the bravest birds came to it now.

But Milly wasn't sitting underneath the bird table and she didn't come when Tia called, like she usually did. She was nowhere to be seen.

"Milly! Milly!" Tia called anxiously. She ran down the garden to look over the back fence into Mr Jackson's garden. Milly liked it over there. Mr Jackson had a goldfish pond. She had climbed the fence at the side of the garden, too, but the people next door had a spaniel called Max, and he had barked at Milly so loudly that she'd jumped straight down again.

Just as Tia reached the back fence and looked through the trellis on the top, there was a splashing sound and a horrified yowl. Then something bounded across Mr Jackson's garden. A small, bedraggled thing, trailing long streamers of green weed.

"That cat of yours is after my goldfish!" Mr Jackson shouted crossly to Tia. "Little menace!"

Milly jumped on to Mr Jackson's compost bin and then up on to the fence, where Tia reached up and grabbed her. She shuddered at the clammy wet fur – Milly was soaking.

"I'm really sorry!" Tia gasped to the old man. "We'll keep her inside!"

"We'll have to," she murmured to Milly, as she carried her down the garden. "Maybe we'd better lock the catflap, so you can only go out when one of us with you. I know you won't like that much, but I'm not going to let anyone steal you!"

Tia was quite right. Milly was most unimpressed with being shut inside. She always followed Tia and Christy when they went out into the garden.

55

She would chase the football, and sometimes Tia carried her up on to their climbing frame. Christy had forgiven her for shredding Owly now, and she would dance down the garden trailing bits of string for Milly to pounce on. But sometimes Milly wanted to go outside on her own, too. It wasn't the same watching the birds from the kitchen windowsill.

Often she sat in the front window instead, especially in the afternoon, when she knew that Tia and Christy would soon be home. People sometimes pointed at her, and Milly could tell that they were saying nice things. One blond-haired man seemed to walk past the house quite often, just to see her. He always stopped and looked at her for ages. And at the other cat, the one that lived across the road.

Milly liked to stare at the other cat as well. But he usually pretended not to see her.

"Look, Christy, Milly's watching for us again," Tia pointed to Milly, sitting in the front window, and Milly leaped for the back of the sofa. She would jump from there to the arm, and then on to the floor to meet them at the front door.

"Nice cat!" There was a young man with blond hair walking slowly past their house on the way to his van. He was jingling the keys in his hand, and he smiled at Tia and Christy. "Is she yours? Does she always run and meet you like that?"

Tia smiled back. She loved
it when people admired
Milly. "Yes," she
said proudly.
"She's
beautiful.
What is she,
a Bengal?"

"Yes, she's four months old," Tia said.

The man smiled again and walked
over to his blue van, which was parked
further up the road.

Mum hurried up behind them.
"Who was that you were talking to?"
she asked.

"Oh – well, he was asking about
Milly," Tia said, frowning. She hadn't
really thought about it, but the man
was a stranger, of course. "He seemed

nice…" she added.

"No, he wasn't," Christy said firmly.
"*I* didn't like him."

"Oh, don't be silly, Christy," Tia
muttered, as Mum started to tell her
off for chatting to people she didn't
know.

"You were just coming, Mum. You
were almost with us," Tia muttered.
But she had a horrible feeling now
that Mum and Christy were right.
She shouldn't have spoken to him. She
sighed. "I suppose we shouldn't tell
people Milly's a Bengal, should we?
In case someone tries to steal her."

Mum put an arm around her
shoulder. "I'm sure that won't happen,
Tia. But next time, just say that I'm the
person to ask, and come and get me!

Come on, let's get in the house. Milly's probably having a fit by now."

Tia had hoped that Milly would get used to staying inside, but the kitten still took every chance she could to sneak out. And she moved so fast she was very good at it.

One lunchtime, when Mum was just heading out for work, Milly slipped round her legs, aiming for the open door. But Mum swooped down and caught her just before she could escape.

"No, sweetie. I know you don't like staying inside, but it's to keep you safe." Mum sighed. "Hopefully the police will catch those awful cat thieves soon.

It's been weeks. You stay there, and I'll be back later with Tia and Christy."

Crossly, Milly prowled back into the living room and jumped up on to the windowsill, watching Mum hurry away down the street. She hated it when they all went out. There was nothing to do. The cat on the other side of the road wasn't even sitting in his window for her to look at.

And she was hungry. She uncurled herself, jumped down and wandered out into the kitchen to see if there was some food left in her bowl. There wasn't.

Milly stalked over to the cat flap and glared at it. She didn't understand why it didn't work any more. It would let her back in from the garden, but now it would never let her out. She pawed at it, just in case, but it still didn't work. It rattled though, which was a good noise, so Milly pawed it again. This time, the catflap shook, and Milly got a delicious whiff of fresh garden air as the flap opened inwards a little way. Then it clicked shut again.

Milly stared at it. It had definitely been a bit open. She banged at it harder this time, and it flew open a little more.

Enough for her to stick her paw in and stop it clicking closed.

Purring with excitement, the kitten wriggled her other paw into the gap and then poked her nose in too, flipping the cat flap all the way up, so she could jump out. She stared back at it triumphantly as she stood on the doorstep, and then she pranced out into the garden.

It was sunny and warm, and everything smelled good. Milly padded across the patio, sniffing here and there, and glancing up at the birds that circled and twittered overhead.

It was the smell of the wheelie bins that made her go down the side path. She was hungry, and although the smell wasn't quite right, there was definitely food in there somewhere. She pattered curiously down the path and sniffed around the bottom of the bins. She was just considering trying to scramble up on to the top of one when next-door's dog, Max, came galloping down the garden on his side of the fence, barking his head off.

Milly shot down the path like a rocket, her tail fluffing up. She remembered Max, all big teeth and flying ears. She wasn't sure if he could get through the fence, but she wasn't going to wait around to find out. She bounded into the front garden and jumped up on to the wall. She then licked her paws furiously, swiping them over her ears. She felt hot and bothered and cross, and washing helped – a little.

The sun was warm, and slowly her tail smoothed down again. Milly's eyes half-closed as she watched the cars going past.

One of the cars stopped, a blue van that she was sure she had seen before. A young man with blond hair got out. Milly pricked up her ears. She had seen him before. He always stopped to admire her in the window. She pretended not to notice the man as he walked up the street, and she gave him a haughty look as he made friendly kissy noises at her.

But she couldn't hold out for long.

She padded
gracefully down
the wall to let
the man stroke
her ears and
tickle her under
the chin.

Milly didn't
even mind
when he picked her up – she liked to
be cuddled.

But then he locked his hand tightly
around the scruff of her neck and
hurried down the road with her. He
opened the back of his blue van and
stuffed her into a cat carrier.

And then he drove away while Milly
howled and scrabbled and fought to
get out.

Chapter Five

"Oh! Milly isn't in the window," Tia said, sounding surprised.

"Maybe she heard Christy singing and went to the door already," Mum suggested. "I bet the whole street heard her."

But there was no kitten rubbing lovingly around their ankles when Mum opened the front door.

Tia hurried into the kitchen to see if Milly was waiting by her food bowl. There was no sign of her at all. "Where is she?" she asked anxiously. "Did you shut her in upstairs, Mum?"

"No… She was definitely getting under my feet when I left," Mum said. "Unless she managed to shut herself in somewhere. Go and check, you two."

Tia and Christy raced upstairs, opening every door and calling frantically. Tia even looked in their wardrobe.

"Milly won't be in there!" Christy told her, but Tia shook her head.

"You never know. Remember when she got shut in the kitchen cupboard?"

"She only went in there because that's where the bag of cat food is,"

Christy pointed out.

But all the cupboards were empty, and they hurried back downstairs.

Mum was starting to get worried. "I've looked everywhere down here," she murmured. "You didn't unlock the cat flap, did you?"

Tia shook her head, glancing at the cat flap. Then she frowned. "Hey, it's not closed properly." She crouched down next to it. It was definitely open, just a little – the flap balanced against the frame. Tia gulped. "She's gone out."

"But it was locked," Mum protested. "How can she have gone out?"

"Look." Tia pointed. "It's still locked, but the lock's only a bit of plastic, Mum. It stops the door opening out, but Milly's so clever, she didn't open it outwards – she pulled it *in*. And then she squeezed under the flap."

Tia unlocked the back door and ran out into the garden. "Milly! Milly!" she called, hoping to see a toffee-gold kitten come darting through the grass. But all she heard was Max, whining next door.

"She's gone…" Tia whispered, her heart thumping so hard it almost hurt. "Someone's taken her." She knew that it was silly – Milly could be in Mr Jackson's garden again, chasing the fish. Or messing about in that garden with all the brambles a few doors down. There was nothing to say that she'd been catnapped. But somehow Tia knew. She just knew.

Milly peered out of the wire cage. The man had tipped her out of the carrier, and she had felt so dazed and dizzy after the car journey that she had simply curled up in the corner with her eyes shut. But now that she was feeling a little better she was trying to understand where she was and what was happening.

Her cage was small – not all that much bigger than the carrier had been – and there was a tatty blanket

in it, a litter tray and a water bowl.
There was a food bowl, too, but it
was empty. The cage was stacked on
top of another one and there were
several more all round the shed. The
whole place was grubby and cold, and
it smelled as though the litter trays
weren't emptied often enough. It was
dark, too – the only window was dirty
and hardly let in any light.

But the strangest thing was that
there were three other cats. Milly
hadn't seen that many since she'd
come to live with Tia and Christy.
Occasionally she would see one of the
neighbourhood cats prowling through
her garden, which she hated. But there
wasn't a lot she could do about it, except
scrabble her paws on the window.

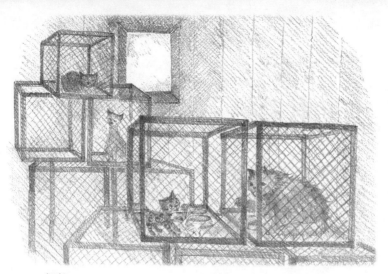

There was a cat in the cage right next to her, just on the other side of the wire. He was bigger than her, and he had a fat, squashed face and a lot of long fur in a strange blue-grey colour. He hissed angrily at Milly, and she took a step back and nearly fell over.

The big blue Persian hissed again and shot out a fat paw, scraping it down the side of the wire with a screechy clatter.

Milly's tail fluffed up to twice its usual size, and she hissed and spat back. She might be small, but she was angry.

She had been stolen and stuffed in a box, and now she was shut up here.

The Persian was still hissing, but crawling backwards now, his golden-orange eyes fixed on hers. They glared at each other, both of them refusing to back down.

As Milly watched him edge up against the side of his cage she decided that there wasn't much point in making a fuss. He was there and she was here, neither of them could get out – that was what they should be worrying about.

She let out a last little growl and curled herself up on the blanket, wondering how she was going to get home to Tia.

"Anything?" Mum asked, as Tia came in from the garden. She had been out to call for Milly again while Mum and Christy went to ask Mr Jackson if he'd seen the kitten, and Max's owners too. No one had seen her, though.

Tia rubbed her eyes, trying not to cry. She didn't want to scare Christy. "Do you think someone took her?" she whispered to Mum.

Mum hugged her. "No, Tia, I'm sure she's just gone exploring. Don't worry."

But Tia *was* worried. Milly never went far. Whenever Tia called her, there'd always be a scrabbling on the other side of the fence and a little whiskery golden face would appear over the top. "Can we go and look up and down the road?" she begged.

They searched their street and the next couple of streets, calling for Milly and asking people if they'd spotted her. And they kept going until it got too dark to see.

Mum said Milly would probably come back when she got hungry, but the kitten still hadn't returned by bedtime. Christy climbed the ladder to Tia's top bunk, and the sisters curled up together.

"She'll come back tomorrow, won't she?" Christy asked.

Tia tried to sound confident. "Oh yes." *Please let it be true*, she thought. "We'll probably find her in her basket when we come down in the morning."

"She could be there now!" Christy clutched at Tia's pyjamas. "We should go downstairs and see!"

"No… Not yet," Tia murmured.
She wasn't sure she could manage not
to cry if they didn't find their lovely
kitten.

"I really miss her…" Christy said
sleepily.

"Me too," Tia sniffed. "But she'll
be back tomorrow," she said, trying
to convince herself.

Chapter Six

But the next morning there was no
Milly yowling for her breakfast. It
seemed so unfair to have to go to school
– all Tia wanted to do was search for
Milly. It was Friday. Nothing important
happened at school on Fridays.

As she trailed into the playground,
her friend Lucy came running over.

"Hi, Tia! Hey, what's the matter?"

"Milly," Tia gulped, swallowing back tears. "She's disappeared. And I can't help thinking someone's kidnapped her. Remember I told you about those cat thieves?"

Lucy's eyes widened. "Oh no! How long's she been gone for?"

"She wasn't there when we got home yesterday. She managed to get out of her cat flap even though it was locked."

Lucy frowned. "I don't think Mittens would ever do anything like that. What makes you think she's been stolen?"

Tia sighed. "It's just a feeling I've got… I know that sounds stupid."

"No…" Lucy said thoughtfully. "I know what you mean. When Mittens was lost, I was sure she'd come back. She was gone for more than a week, and Mum told me maybe I should give up, but I didn't."

"I forgot about that! It was in the summer holidays, wasn't it? How did you find her?" Tia asked eagerly.

"We made loads of posters and stuck them on lamp posts, and I put leaflets through the door of every house in our road, asking them to check their sheds. And that's where somebody found her! It was just lucky that it was a leaky shed and there was a puddle of water, otherwise Mittens would have died," Lucy added, her voice shaking a little.

"Posters…" Tia said thoughtfully. "And leaflets. Right. We'll make some tonight."

"What about this one?" Tia said to Dad, pointing to one of the photos of Milly on the screen.

"Mmmm." Dad nodded. "But she's more recognizable from the side, don't you think? Because of her lovely spots."

"Look!" Christy said. "That's the one Mum took when Milly climbed into the cupboard!"

Tia enlarged the photo and smiled. Milly was peering out, looking worried. They'd actually moved the cat food to the top cupboard after her first cat-food raid. And Mum had even started keeping the food in a tin instead of a bag. But Milly was just too clever. She'd even managed to hook the lid open with her claws.

"She's so naughty…" Mum sighed.

"Mum!" Tia looked up at her. "Aren't you sad she's missing?"

"Of course I am, Tia! But she *is* naughty!"

"I suppose you wish we had a better-behaved cat instead!" Tia said, her voice choked with tears.

"I didn't mean that at all," Mum tried to say, but Tia was too upset to listen.

"You're glad she's gone!" she sobbed.

"Tia!" Mum snapped, her voice

sharp enough to jolt Tia out of her fit of crying. "Sweetheart, that's just silly. Yes, I get cross with Milly when she's naughty, but she's a kitten! Kittens do silly things, it's what we signed up for! Especially when we agreed to have a Bengal." She put her arm round Tia's shoulder. "Do you think you're the only one who read that book on Bengal cats?"

Tia gaped at her. She hadn't realized Mum had read the book too.

"When I'm at home with her in the mornings, she follows me around, you know." Mum sniffed. "And I'm always having to rescue her from the washing machine. It's a wonder I've never actually put it on with her in it! I love her too, Tia, and we will do our absolute best to find her."

"Sorry," Tia murmured. Somehow knowing that Mum was really missing Milly helped.

Dad smiled. "She's a little terror, isn't she? But nobody wants a better-behaved cat, Tia. We want *our* cat. Now I think this photo of her in the garden is the best. What shall we say on the poster?"

Milly stared at the door, wondering when the man would come to bring their food. He'd fed them that morning, but the food hadn't been the same kind she had at home. She'd left it for a while, but then finally eaten it – she'd been too hungry not to.

She had tried to dart out of the cage when the man put her food bowl in, but he'd batted her away. She felt hopeless – she couldn't see how she was ever going to get out of here. And she was hungry again.

Tia always fed her at about this time of day. Where *was* Tia? Milly had been hoping that Tia would come and take her away from this horrible place.

She began to wail, over and over again. The Persian cat didn't join in, he just stayed in the corner of his cage, sulking. But the other two cats started to howl too.

The door banged open, and the man stamped in, scowling. "Shut up!" he yelled, hitting the front of the cage.

Milly let out a frightened little whimper. No one had ever shouted at her like that before. People had been cross or snapped, "Milly, no!" But this was different. She cowered at the back of the cage as he shoved in a fresh bowl of food. She didn't even think about trying to escape this time. She didn't want to go any closer to the man than she had to.

"I'm glad it's Saturday and we can be out looking for Milly," Tia said to Lucy. Her mum had texted Lucy's the night before to ask if Lucy could come and help.

"That's a brilliant photo," Lucy said, as she gave Tia some sellotape to stick the poster to a lamp post. "Anyone who sees Milly will definitely recognize her."

Tia sighed. "I don't think anyone will see her, though. I still reckon it was those catnappers Laura told me about. Mum did ring the police, and they said they'd make a note of it, but there wasn't a lot to go on. Actually, do you mind if we run back and ask Mum if we can go and tell Laura what's happened? I want to warn her to keep Charlie safe."

"Good idea," Lucy agreed. "If the catnappers did take Milly, I bet they saw Charlie too. They might come back, mightn't they?"

"Exactly." Tia shuddered.

They hurried back down the road to meet Tia's mum and Christy, who were doing the lamp posts at that end. Mum had told the girls they could go further up the road as long as they stayed where she could see them. Dad had gone to the street that ran behind theirs, in case Milly had jumped over the back fence.

"Mum! Can we go and tell Laura what happened? I want to warn her to keep Charlie in."

"Oh, Tia… I'm sure it's nothing to do with catnappers," Mum said, patting her shoulder. "Milly's just wandered off. Cats do!"

"Please?"

"Well, OK. But don't bother Laura for long."

Tia and Lucy crossed over the road, and rang Laura's bell.

"Hello! I've just seen you from upstairs, putting up posters." Laura frowned. "Milly's not lost, is she?"

"Yes." Tia gulped. "Actually, I'm sure she's been stolen. There was a man asking me about her, just a couple of days ago…"

Laura gasped. "Youngish? Short blond hair? With a blue van?"

"I don't know about the van…" Tia started to say. "Hang on, yes, there was a van…" She scowled to herself, wishing she could remember. It just hadn't seemed important at the time. "I think it was blue. You saw him too, then?"

"Yes! He was asking me about Charlie. He was nice, he said my cat looked very special, and I was all set to say Charlie was a Bengal. Then I remembered that newspaper article, and I just smiled at him and went inside. I felt a bit guilty afterwards.

I was rude…"

"He was nice to me too," Tia whispered sadly. "If he was asking about Charlie, that's not just chance, is it? He's a cat thief, and Milly really has been stolen." Tia's eyes filled with tears. "He'll sell her to someone else, and we'll never get her back!"

Chapter Seven

Milly flattened her ears. She could hear the man coming. She gave a small, nervous mew. He frightened her.

He had a pile of food bowls in one hand, but in the other he was holding a cat carrier. What was happening? Then she suddenly realized – perhaps he was going to take her home! She purred, hoping she was the one he had brought the carrier for.

She stood nicely as he opened the cage door, and let him pick her up and put her in, though usually she would scrabble and fight.

"Who's being a good girl," he murmured in the sort of voice that Tia would use. Milly still didn't like him, but at least he was carrying her carefully. She had expected him to put her back in the van. But instead he put the carrier down indoors somewhere and left her.

What was happening? Why had he put her in the carrier if he wasn't going to take her home? Milly mewed worriedly, but she didn't howl like she had before. If she was noisy, she was sure the man would shout at her again.

At last, she heard him coming back.

He was talking to someone else, a woman, and his voice was soft.

"Yes, she's lovely. Unfortunately her owner couldn't keep her. The old lady had to go into hospital, you see, so she asked me to find her a new home. She's very reasonably priced for a Bengal."

Milly tensed as he undid the clips on the front door of the carrier, and then he reached in and scooped her out. She did her best not to hiss, but she wanted to, and the fur rose up all along her back.

"Oh dear, she doesn't look very happy." The woman frowned. "She's so pretty, though. Do you have her pedigree?"

"I don't have the pedigree at the moment – with being in hospital, her owner was a bit frantic. But it's very good."

"Can I hold her?" the woman asked, and she took Milly, stroking her softly. The woman seemed nice – or at any rate, a lot nicer than the man. Milly relaxed a little. She didn't know who this person was, but perhaps she was going to take her back to Tia.

"Oh…" The lady ran her hand down Milly's tail. "There's something wrong with her tail."

"What?" The man's voice was cross

again, and Milly flinched and pressed herself against the woman's coat.

"Look – it's bent over."

"Well, that doesn't matter, does it? Seeing how reasonable the price is."

"I don't know. If there's something wrong with her…" The woman held Milly out to the man. "I hope I haven't wasted your time."

Milly looked up at her, realizing that she wasn't going to take her away from here, and let out a despairing yowl. The man snatched her and stuffed her into the carrier, slamming the wire door angrily. He looked furious – and the woman appeared very glad to be leaving.

Milly was worried that he might come back and shout at her again.

But there was a loud bang, like a door shutting, and heavy footsteps went thudding away upstairs.

After a few minutes she felt brave enough to come closer to the wire door and look out. The room was a kitchen, a bit like Tia's, and the carrier seemed to be on a table. Milly pressed her nose up against the wire and then jumped back as it moved.

He hadn't shut the door! He had only slammed it – he hadn't twisted the catches to hold it in place! Milly nudged the door with her nose, harder and harder, and it swung open. She jumped out on to the table. She had to get away from here, as quickly as she could. She looked over at the back door, but there was no cat flap.

There was a window, though. Above the sink, like at home. And it was open, just a little.

Milly stood at the edge of the table, her back legs tensed, ready to spring. There were glasses and plates stacked by the sink, and if she banged into them, he might come. She had to be quiet as well as quick. She leaped right into the sink, and some knives and forks jingled under her paws. But there was no thunder of footsteps on the stairs. Hurriedly, she climbed up to the windowsill. She was free!

"What did the police say?" Tia asked. She'd been hovering by her mum the whole while she'd been on the phone.

"Well, this time they did seem to take it a bit more seriously. They said they'd pass on all the information."

"They think Milly *was* stolen, then?" Tia said, her voice eager. "They'll find her?"

Mum sighed. "Look, Tia, the police will do the best they can. But there isn't a lot to go on, is there?"

"I suppose not," Tia sat down at the table, her legs feeling wobbly. Then she frowned. "If they haven't got much to go on, we have to find them some more evidence, Mum! Lucy said we should put posters up in the shops near her. There's a newsagent's with a board – she says loads of people go and read the ads on it. Please!"

"All right. It's quite a walk, though. Dad's taken the car to drive round and look for Milly."

"I don't mind!" Tia assured her.

Mum sighed. "Have you printed out some more posters?"

Tia picked up a pile from the end of the table and waved them at her.

"Now, you two go into the newsagent's, and I'll go and ask if I can put a poster up in the library," Mum said. She was sounding a bit weary. Christy had whinged most of the way, saying she was sick of walking. Tia had tried to explain that it was all because they were trying to find Milly, but when Christy was tired she wasn't easy to persuade.

Tia walked up to the counter and the young woman smiled at her. "Are you after some sweets?" she asked.

Tia shook her head. "We came to ask if we could put this up on your board." She held out a poster. "It's our kitten, you see. She's missing."

"Oh no! Look at her, isn't she lovely!"

Tia swallowed back tears. "We think she might have been stolen. There was an article about it in the local paper."

"I remember. Is your cat one of those Bengals, then?"

"Yes. A man was hanging around asking about her, and one day we got back home from school and she was gone."

The woman nodded. "The board's over there. You can move a couple of the leaflets around if you need space."

"Thank you very much!" Tia went over to the board while Christy eyed the sweets hungrily. It was covered in leaflets, some of them curling at the edges as though they'd been there forever. Tia started to unpin a few of them so she could make room for her poster. Most of them were adverts for things people wanted to sell – lawnmowers and pushchairs. Then Tia stopped, staring at the card she'd just taken down.

Pedigree cats for sale. All breeds. Reasonably priced.

And there was a phone number.

How could someone be selling all breeds of cat? Breeders like Helen only bred one sort. No one could have all the different breeds.

Unless they were stealing them.

"What's the matter?" the woman called to Tia. "You look like you've seen a ghost."

Tia walked back over to the counter. "You don't remember who put this up, do you?" she asked, not very hopefully.

The woman looked down at the card. "Oh, I see. You're thinking—"

"It could be them, couldn't it?" Tia gasped. She was desperate for a clue. Anything that might help them track Milly down.

The woman sniffed. "As it happens, I do know who put that up, and I wouldn't be surprised if he *was* a cat thief. He's rude. I wish he didn't come in here, but he picks up his motorcycle magazine every week. Some special order."

Tia stared at her. "So – have you got his address then?" she whispered.

The woman looked uncomfortable. "Well, yes… I mean, I shouldn't give it out. Just don't say I gave it to you, will you?" She pulled out a big folder and flicked through. "Here, look. That's him. But hang on, you can't go over there on your own! Where's your mum and dad?"

"It's all right," Tia said. "My mum's just at the library – I'll get her. Seventeen Emwell Road. Thanks!"

She grabbed Christy's hand, and hauled her out of the shop. "I think we're about to get Milly back! We have to find Mum… Come on."

They raced up the steps to the library and shoved open the door.

Mum was in the queue, and there were loads of people in front of her.

"I won't be too long, Tia," Mum said, as Tia came up to her.

"But I've found them!" Tia cried. "The catnappers!"

"What?" Mum stared at her, and some of the people in the line looked round curiously.

"There was an ad for pedigree cats for sale in the newsagent's. It has to be them! And I've got the address."

"Oh, Tia, I know you're desperate to find Milly, but you're jumping to conclusions." Mum shook her head.

"Why won't you ever believe me?" Tia said furiously. "I'm going there now!" She turned and marched out, Christy scampering after her. She didn't even look back to see if Mum was following. She just had to find Milly.

Chapter Eight

Milly threaded her way through the overgrown front garden and squeezed under the rickety wooden gate. She darted a glance back to the house, but the man wasn't chasing her. Still, she wanted to get further away. Then she would find Tia. She set off down the pavement, sniffing at the dandelions and the parked cars. It was when she

reached the end of the street, where
it met another, larger road, that she
realized finding her home was going to
be harder than she'd thought. She had
expected to somehow know which way
to go. But coming here in a van, she
had lost her sense of direction.

She set off along one road, but it
didn't feel good. Milly turned
uncertainly and hurried back.
The other way felt as though it
led home.

Milly plodded
on, trying to sense
the right direction.
She wasn't used to walking so far and
the pavements were hard. Her paws
hurt. Worst of all, she wasn't really sure
she was getting any closer to Tia.

Wearily, she jumped up on to a
low wall for a rest. Another cat had
scent-marked the garden beyond the
wall, and Milly peered down nervously.
The cat didn't seem to be around. She
curled herself into a tense little ball
and let her eyes close. She was so tired.

Suddenly, Milly's eyes shot open, and
she nearly fell off the wall. A ginger cat
was in the garden below her, hissing
furiously. His fur fluffed up so much
that he looked four
times as big as her.

Milly scrambled backwards, her tail straight up, all the fur sticking out like a brush. She hissed at the ginger cat, but he was much bigger than she was. Milly backed herself up to the end of the wall and then sprang down on to the pavement, racing away as fast as she could.

"It's this way," Tia panted, hauling Christy along behind her.

"We should wait for Mum!" Christy wailed. "I can't see her, Tia! We aren't supposed to go where we can't see Mum! We'll get in trouble!"

"I don't care! I'm going to find Milly. Look, this is Emwell Road!"

Tia stopped, gasping for breath. What if the man who took Milly saw her and Christy? He'd probably recognize them. "Be like spies, all right? We don't want the catnappers to catch us."

Tia pulled Christy in close to the wall and they began to creep along, looking for number seventeen.

"This is it," Tia murmured, a little way up the road. "Oh! The van!" She squeezed Christy's hand and pointed. "Laura saw a blue van when the man was asking about Charlie."

"Tia!" Mum was running up the road after them, looking furious. "How could you run off like that? You crossed roads! You know you're not allowed!"

"Mum, look!" Tia grabbed her arm, towing her towards the van. "Look! It's the catnappers!"

Mum frowned. "Oh… Is that the van Laura talked about?"

"Yes! And this is the road where the man who put up that advert lives. It's got to be him, hasn't it?"

Mum nodded slowly. "All right. Don't you dare go in there, Tia! I'm going to call that number the police gave me. It's starting to look as though you're right."

"Have a look at these." The policewoman held out her mobile phone, and Tia stared at it eagerly. It had been so hard to wait for news. Tia had wanted to stay outside the house in Emwell Road, but Mum had said they'd better go home. They didn't want to get in the way when the police came.

"We might make that man suspicious if we're hanging around," she had pointed out to Tia. "We don't want him moving the cats."

Tia knew she was right, but she hated to walk away when she was so sure that Milly was somewhere in that house.

It had only been a few hours until a police car drew up outside their house that evening, but it felt like Tia had been waiting for days.

"Is Milly one of these?" PC Ryan flicked through the photos – a Persian, and what looked like another Bengal, but with a marbled, stripey coat, and another cat Tia didn't recognize.

"No…" Tia's voice shook. "Look, there's an empty cage next to this one. He's already sold her!"

PC Ryan frowned. "Maybe. But he was definitely showing a spotted Bengal kitten to someone this morning. Another lady phoned us, saying that she'd been to see a kitten, and she suspected she might have been stolen. Perhaps your Milly got out."

"Milly is very good at getting in and out of places," Mum agreed hopefully. "If any cat could, it would be her, wouldn't it, Tia…"

But Tia wasn't listening. She dashed away upstairs to her room and scrambled up her ladder to hide in her bed. She couldn't bear it. They were too late, and Milly was gone.

Milly kept walking all afternoon even though she was so tired she stumbled. The light was starting to fade now, and it was getting colder. Someone was walking along the road towards her with a dog, and Milly darted under a parked car to hide.

Even when the dog had gone by, she didn't want to move. At least under the car she was out of the wind, and she couldn't smell any other cats. She would just stay here for a little while, until she felt better. Milly dozed, her eyelids flickering and her paws twitching as the ginger cat chased after her. It was chasing her further and further away from Tia…

She hissed and startled awake, not sure where she was. It was now bright daylight, she realized as she peered out from under the parked car. She must have slept there all night, worn out from her long walk.

She stepped cautiously out on to the pavement and stretched herself. Then she heard voices. Children's voices. Not Tia and Christy, she was pretty sure, but still … she would just go and see. Somehow she felt much more hopeful today, with the bright sunshine warming her fur.

It was a playground, and two little

boys were chasing each other round and round. Milly paused at the gate, ready to run.

"Ooooh, look! Mum, look! A kitten!"
The older boy dashed over.

Milly squeaked – she was nervous
after the way that nice man had turned
out not to be nice after all. She shot
underneath the slide and hid there,
shivering.

"Oh, Alfie, you frightened her. She
doesn't know you like Whiskers does.
No, don't try and pull her out, Billy.
She'll come out if she wants to."

The woman's voice was gentle, and
the fur began to lay down flat on Milly's
back again. "She is pretty... Oh!"

"What, Mum?"

"I think she's the kitten on those
posters! You know, we said it was sad
that she was lost. She's called Milly, if
she is that missing kitten."

"And we found her!"

"No, I found her! I saw her first!"

"Shhh! You'll scare her away. We need to ring the number and say she's found. You two watch her, and I'll run and see if I can find a poster. I think I saw one on that lamp post by the gate."

Milly huddled under the slide with two curious little faces staring in. She was feeling a bit better now – the bigger boy had surprised her, that was all. She sniffed at his fingers as he held them out hopefully, and he beamed and patted her head.

"Hello, Milly…"

Milly came out from under the slide a little more. The boy knew her name! She nuzzled his fingers, and he giggled.

"Me too! Me too!" the littler one squeaked, so she rubbed her head against his jeans.

The boys' mother hurried back over. "Good boys… I'm just ringing her owners now…" she said, crouching down beside them. She smiled at Milly as she keyed in the number. "I bet you want to go home, don't you?"

"Tia, love, wake up."

Tia blinked and rubbed at her sticky eyes. They were sore, and she couldn't remember why. And then all at once she did remember and she gave a horrified little gasp.

Mum was standing at the bottom of the bunkbed ladder with Christy next to her. "Tia, why don't you get up and have a shower and get changed? You fell asleep in your clothes last night!"

Tia peered over the edge of her bed. "Milly could be anywhere, Mum. That man isn't telling the police anything, PC Ryan said so. He just says he's looking after the cats for a friend. He must have sold her. We're never going to get Milly back."

"Listen, Dad and I think PC Ryan's right. The man was showing someone a kitten just like Milly yesterday morning. You *know* how sneaky Milly can be! She ran away from him, I'm sure she did. The police have arrested the man, so they'll be able to ask him more questions. Dad's gone to put more posters up around Emwell Road. Do you want to go out looking again after breakfast? Shall we see if Lucy wants to come and help too?"

Tia sniffed and nodded, and Mum reached up awkwardly to hug her round the ladder. "Oh, that's my phone. Maybe it's Dad." She dug it out of her pocket. "Hello?" She listened for a moment and then she gasped, shaking Tia's shoulder. "Someone's found her! She *must* have escaped! She's not even that far away." Mum held the phone back to her ear. "In the park between here and school. Oh, thank you so much, we'll be there in a few minutes. Tia, come back!"

But Tia had already jumped down the ladder, and Christy was racing after her.

Milly had stopped listening to the little boys as they told her how nice she was and what soft fur she had. She could hear something. A voice…

It was Christy! "Tia, wait for me!"

"Come on, Christy! This is where Milly is, they said on the phone."

Milly jumped right over the little boy's knees and raced for the park gate.

"She's there! Look!" Christy squealed.

"Milly!" Tia crouched down and the kitten bounded up to her, purring delightedly. "Oh, we were so worried!" She stood up, cradling Milly in her arms like a baby.

"Thank you for phoning us!" Tia said shyly to the woman with the two little boys.

The woman smiled. "I'm just glad we saw her. She's beautiful, isn't she?"

Tia smiled back. "She's the most beautiful kitten ever."

Christy danced round her sister. "We found you! Mum, look, here's Milly!"

"She's fine!" Tia called, as she turned to see Mum hurrying towards them.

"Better than fine," her mum said, gently tickling Milly under the chin. "You little darling, did you run away from that man, hmmm?"

"The most beautiful kitten ever *and* the cleverest!" Tia sighed happily. It felt like she could breathe properly for the first time since Milly had disappeared. There had been a horrible lump of fear stuck in her throat all that time. "We got you back," she whispered, rubbing her cheek over the top of the kitten's head, and Milly purred so hard she shook all over.

Lucky Escape for Kidnapped Kitten!

Reunited: Tia and Christy are delighted to have their kitten back!

A Bengal kitten was returned to her owners after escaping from the clutches of a local cat thief. The cat, named Milly, was stolen last week. The thief intended to sell her to unsuspecting customers.

Fortunately, her dedicated owner, Tia, put up posters and undertook detective work following our recent article about catnapping. Milly was found at a local playground, having somehow escaped from the thief. And, thanks to the posters, the lady who found her knew who to call!

Tia and her younger sister, Christy, were thrilled to have Milly returned safely. As Tia told *The Purberry Post*: "I was so frightened when she went missing, but I suppose I should have known she'd escape the catnapper – she's so clever!"

The thief has been caught and is under questioning by the police. Three other pedigree cats found at his home have been returned to their rightful owners.

P U R
Counc
reache
target
shortl
constr
the n
playg
site
Park
prepa
assen
pirate
playg
will
clim
pirat
obsta
"V
excit
buil
fant
faci
Nad
Purt
ama
a c
is
to
proj
S
org
hel
mo
pla
ha
bak
wa
fai
ho
pla
the
be
m

HOLLY WEBB

Holly Webb started out as a children's book editor, and wrote her first series for the publisher she worked for. She has been writing ever since, with over seventy books to her name. Holly lives in Berkshire, with her husband and three young sons. She has a pet cat called Milly, who is always nosying around when Holly is trying to type on her laptop.

For more information
about Holly Webb visit:

www.holly-webb.com